THE EMERALD CITY OF OZ
VOL. 1

ADAPTED FROM
THE BOOK BY
L. FRANK BAUM

Writer: ERIC SHANOWER
Artist: SKOTTIE YOUNG
Colorist: JEAN-FRANCOIS BEAULIEU
Letterer: JEFF ECKLEBERRY

Assistant Editor: DEVIN LEWIS
Editor: SANA AMANAT

Collection Editor: MARK D. BEAZLEY
Associate Managing Editor: ALEX STARBUCK
Editor, Special Projects: JENNIFER GRÜNWALD
Senior Editor, Special Projects: JEFF YOUNGQUIST
Senior Vice President Print, Sales & Marketing: DAVID GABRIEL

Editor in Chief: AXEL ALONSO
Chief Creative Officer: JOE QUESADA
Publisher: DAN BUCKLEY

ABDO
Spotlight

ABDOPUBLISHING.COM

Reinforced library bound edition published in 2015 by Spotlight,
a division of ABDO, PO Box 398166, Minneapolis, Minnesota 55439.
Spotlight produces high-quality reinforced library bound editions for
schools and libraries. Published by agreement with Marvel Characters, Inc.

Printed in the United States of America, North Mankato, Minnesota.
112014
012015

THIS BOOK CONTAINS
RECYCLED MATERIALS

Marvel.com
© 2014 Marvel

LIBRARY OF CONGRESS CATALOGING-IN-PUBLICATION DATA

Shanower, Eric.
  The Emerald City of Oz / writer: Eric Shanower ; artist: Skottie Young. --
Reinforced library bound edition.
      pages cm
  "Marvel."
  Summary: Dorothy's aunt and uncle get acquainted with Oz after they
lose their farm and Ozma invites them to live with her.
  ISBN 978-1-61479-352-6 (vol. 1) -- ISBN 978-1-61479-353-3 (vol. 2) --
ISBN 978-1-61479-354-0 (vol. 3) -- ISBN 978-1-61479-355-7 (vol. 4) -- ISBN
978-1-61479-356-4 (vol. 5)
  1. Graphic novels. [1. Graphic novels. 2. Fantasy.] I. Young, Skottie,
illustrator. II. Baum, L. Frank (Lyman Frank), 1856-1919. Dorothy and the
Wizard in Oz. III. Title.
  PZ7.7.S453Eme 2015
  741.5'973--dc23
                    2014033626

Spotlight

A Division of ABDO
abdopublishing.com

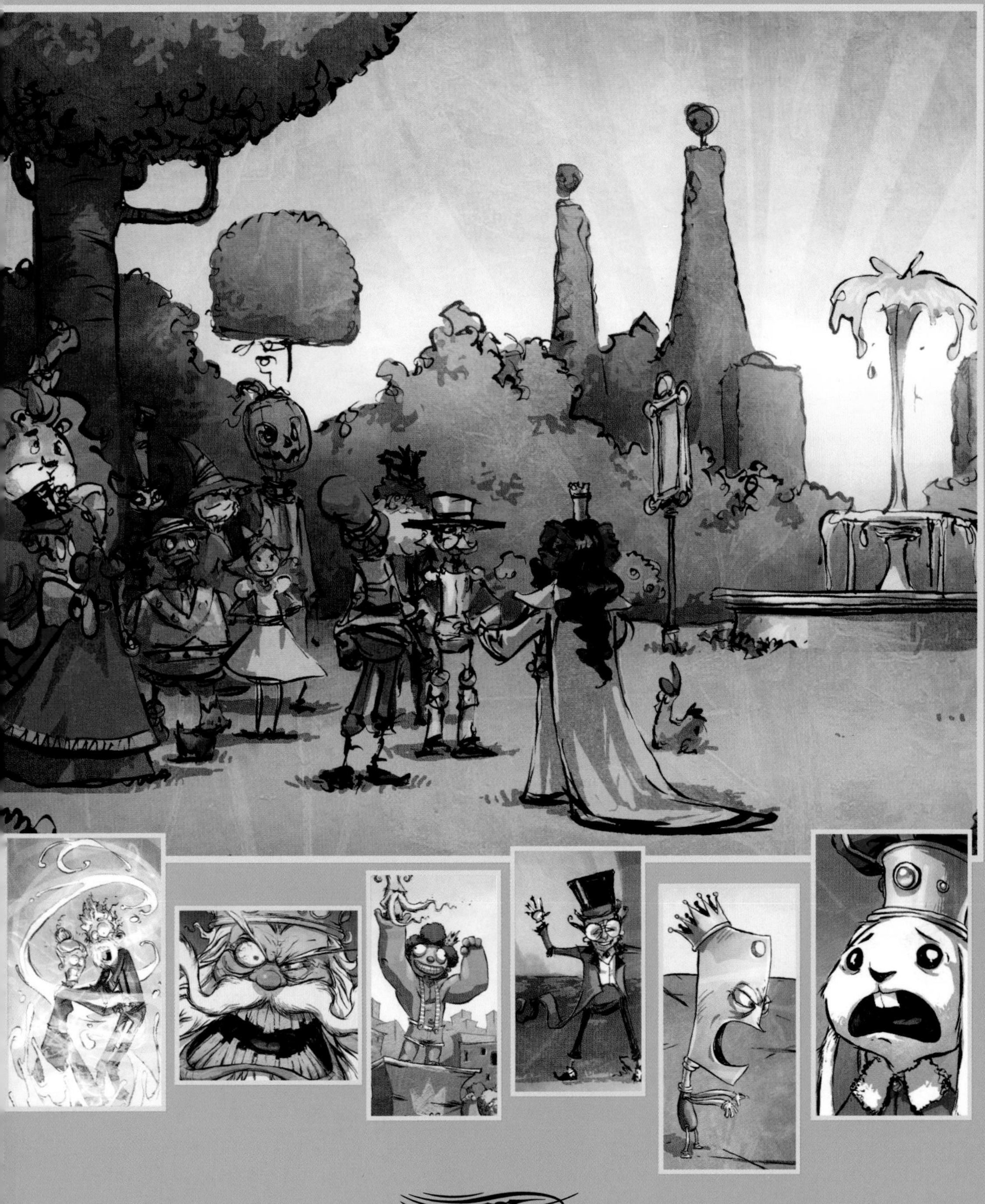

BAAAAAAAAHH!

THE NOME KING, ROQUAT THE RED, WAS IN AN ANGRY MOOD.

BONG!

SEND MY CHIEF STEWARD HERE!

EVERY LITTLE WHILE I WANT TO DO SOMETHING MAGICAL, BUT I *CAN'T* BECAUSE MY MAGIC BELT IS *GONE!* THAT MAKES ME *ANGRY!*

S-SOME PEOPLE ENJOY BEING ANGRY.

BUT NOT ALL THE TIME! IT PREVENTS MY GAINING ANY OTHER PLEASURE IN LIFE!

IF YOUR MAJESTY IS ANGRY BECAUSE YOU WANT TO DO MAGICAL THINGS AND CAN'T, MY ADVICE IS NOT TO WANT TO DO MAGICAL THINGS.

FOOL! I WANT MY MAGIC BELT! A GIRL NAMED DOROTHY, WHO WAS HERE WITH OZMA OF OZ, STOLE IT AND LEFT IT IN THE LAND OF OZ!

SHE CAPTURED IT IN A FAIR FIGHT.

BUT I MUST HAVE IT! *HALF MY POWER* IS GONE WITH THAT BELT!

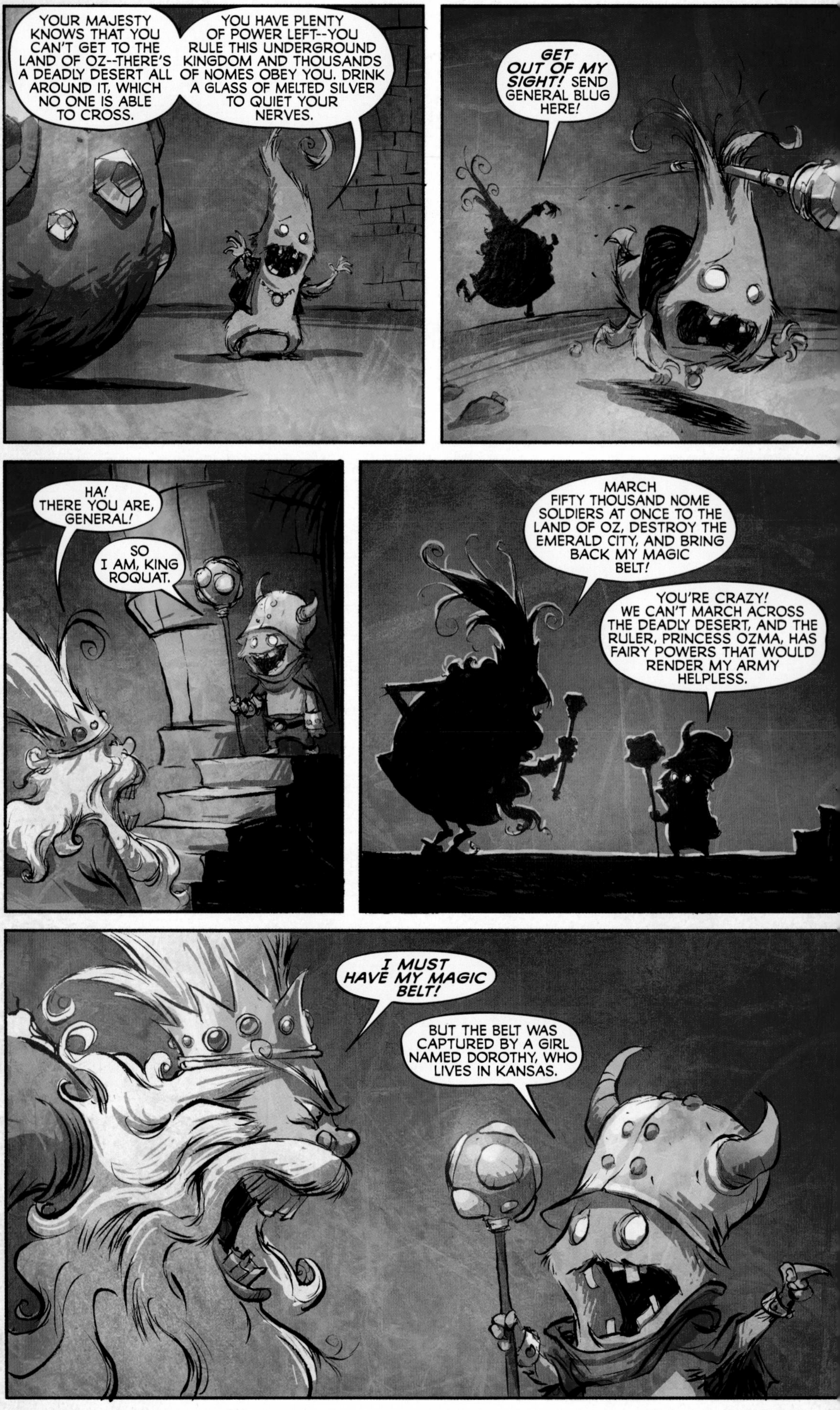
YOUR MAJESTY KNOWS THAT YOU CAN'T GET TO THE LAND OF OZ--THERE'S A DEADLY DESERT ALL AROUND IT, WHICH NO ONE IS ABLE TO CROSS.
YOU HAVE PLENTY OF POWER LEFT--YOU RULE THIS UNDERGROUND KINGDOM AND THOUSANDS OF NOMES OBEY YOU. DRINK A GLASS OF MELTED SILVER TO QUIET YOUR NERVES.
GET OUT OF MY SIGHT! SEND GENERAL BLUG HERE!
HA! THERE YOU ARE, GENERAL!
SO I AM, KING ROQUAT.
MARCH FIFTY THOUSAND NOME SOLDIERS AT ONCE TO DESTROY THE LAND OF OZ, DESTROY THE EMERALD CITY, AND BRING BACK MY MAGIC BELT!
YOU'RE CRAZY! WE CAN'T MARCH ACROSS THE DEADLY DESERT, AND THE RULER, PRINCESS OZMA, HAS FAIRY POWERS THAT WOULD RENDER MY ARMY HELPLESS.
I MUST HAVE MY MAGIC BELT!
BUT THE BELT WAS CAPTURED BY A GIRL NAMED DOROTHY, WHO LIVES IN KANSAS.

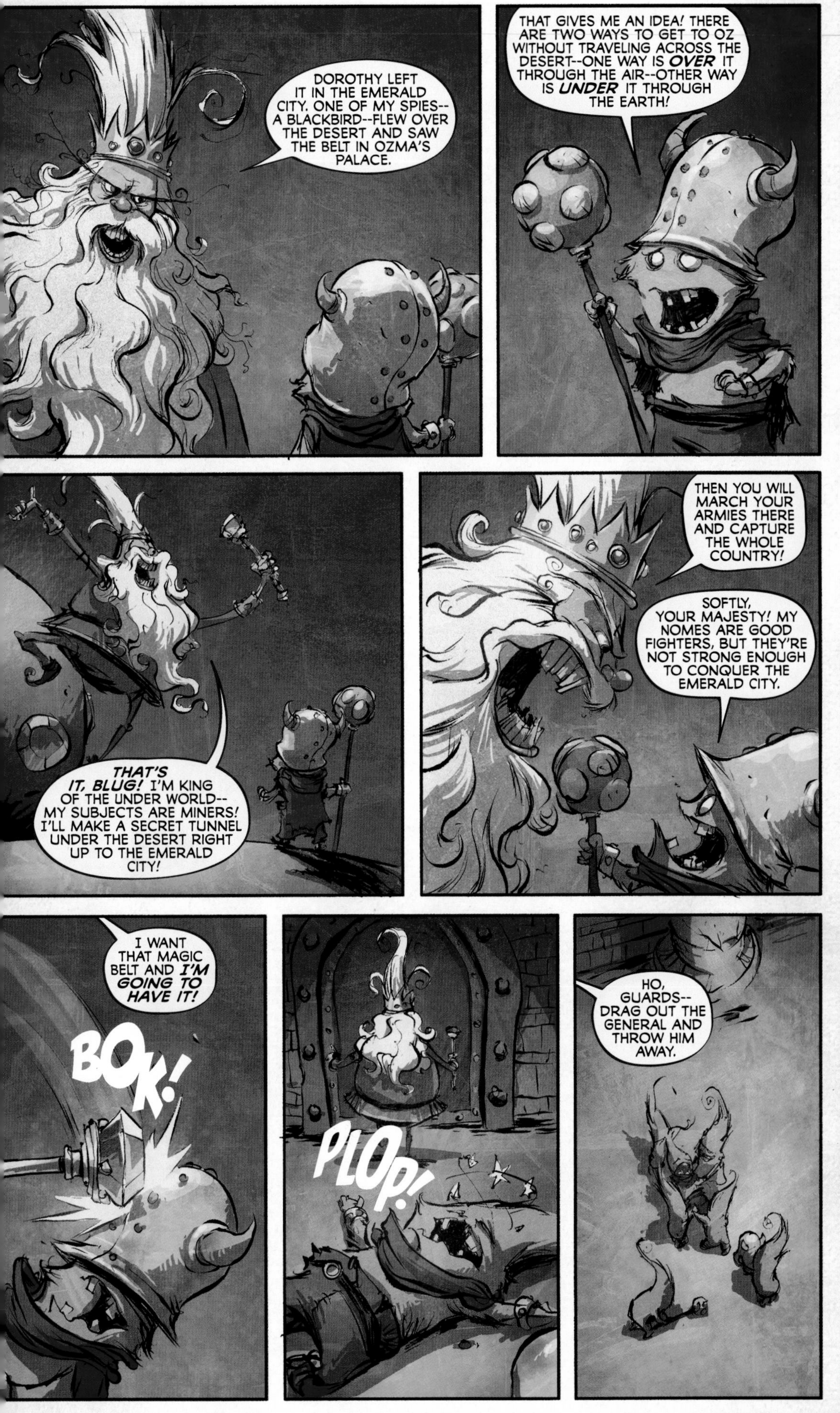
DOROTHY LEFT IT IN THE EMERALD CITY. ONE OF MY SPIES--A BLACKBIRD--FLEW OVER THE DESERT AND SAW THE BELT IN OZMA'S PALACE.
THAT GIVES ME AN IDEA! THERE ARE TWO WAYS TO GET TO OZ WITHOUT TRAVELING ACROSS THE DESERT--ONE WAY IS OVER IT THROUGH THE AIR--OTHER WAY IS UNDER IT THROUGH THE EARTH!
THAT'S IT, BLUG! I'M KING OF THE UNDER WORLD--MY SUBJECTS ARE MINERS! I'LL MAKE A SECRET TUNNEL UNDER THE DESERT RIGHT UP TO THE EMERALD CITY!
THEN YOU WILL MARCH YOUR ARMIES THERE AND CAPTURE THE WHOLE COUNTRY!
SOFTLY, YOUR MAJESTY! MY NOMES ARE GOOD FIGHTERS, BUT THEY'RE NOT STRONG ENOUGH TO CONQUER THE EMERALD CITY.
I WANT THAT MAGIC BELT AND I'M GOING TO HAVE IT!
BOK!
PLOP!
HO, GUARDS--DRAG OUT THE GENERAL AND THROW HIM AWAY.

THE NOME KING SUMMONED HIS ARMY TO ASSEMBLE IN THE GREAT CAVERN.

I HAVE THROWN AWAY GENERAL BLUG BECAUSE HE DIDN'T PLEASE ME! WHO'S NEXT IN COMMAND?

I AM, YOUR MAJESTY-- COLONEL CRINKLE!

I WANT YOU TO MARCH THIS ARMY THROUGH AN UNDERGROUND TUNNEL, WHICH I'M GOING TO BORE, TO THE EMERALD CITY OF OZ.

I WANT YOU TO DESTROY THE OZ PEOPLE AND BRING THEIR GOLD AND JEWELS BACK TO ME. ALSO MY MAGIC BELT. WILL YOU DO THIS, *GENERAL* CRINKLE?

NO, YOUR MAJESTY, IT CAN'T BE DONE.

GUARDS, TAKE GENERAL CRINKLE TO THE TORTURE CHAMBER. THERE YOU WIL SLICE HIM INTO THIN SLICES.

ANYTHING TO OBLIGE YOUR MAJESTY.

AFTERWARD YOU MAY FEED HIM TO THE SEVEN-HEADED DOGS.

NOW, THEN, WHO WILL VOLUNTEER TO LEAD MY HOSTS TO THE EMERALD CITY?

I'D LIKE TO ASK A FEW QUESTIONS, YOUR MAJESTY!

GO AHEAD.

THESE OZ PEOPLE ARE GOOD, AREN'T THEY?

AS APPLE PIE.

AND HAPPY?

AS THE DAY IS LONG.

AND CONTENTED AND PROSPEROUS?

VERY MUCH SO!

YOUR MAJESTY, I'LL BE YOUR GENERAL. I HATE GOOD PEOPLE, I DETEST HAPPY PEOPLE, I'M OPPOSED TO ANY-ONE CONTENTED AND PROSPEROUS.

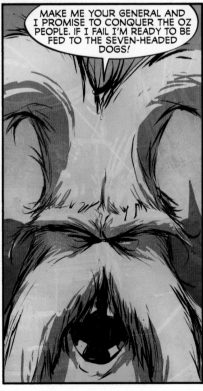

MAKE ME YOUR GENERAL AND I PROMISE TO CONQUER THE OZ PEOPLE. IF I FAIL I'M READY TO BE FED TO THE SEVEN-HEADED DOGS!

VERY GOOD! WHAT IS YOUR NAME, GENERAL?

I'M CALLED GUPH, YOUR MAJESTY.

COME WITH ME TO MY PRIVATE CAVE AND WE'LL TALK.

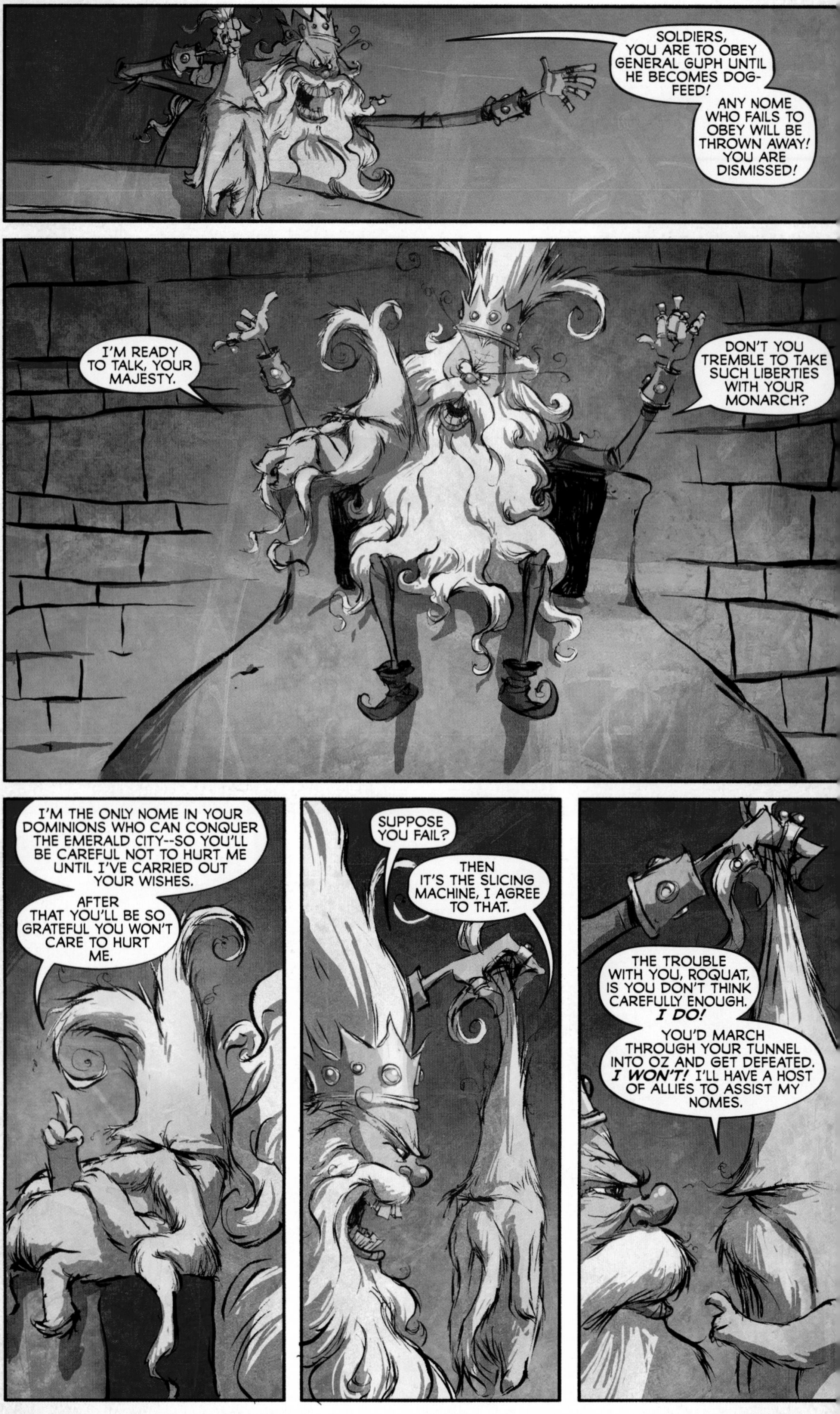
SOLDIERS, YOU ARE TO OBEY GENERAL GUPH UNTIL HE BECOMES DOG-FEED!
ANY NOME WHO FAILS TO OBEY WILL BE THROWN AWAY! YOU ARE DISMISSED!
I'M READY TO TALK, YOUR MAJESTY.
DON'T YOU TREMBLE TO TAKE SUCH LIBERTIES WITH YOUR MONARCH?
I'M THE ONLY NOME IN YOUR DOMINIONS WHO CAN CONQUER THE EMERALD CITY--SO YOU'LL BE CAREFUL NOT TO HURT ME UNTIL I'VE CARRIED OUT YOUR WISHES.
AFTER THAT YOU'LL BE SO GRATEFUL YOU WON'T CARE TO HURT ME.
SUPPOSE YOU FAIL?
THEN IT'S THE SLICING MACHINE, I AGREE TO THAT.
THE TROUBLE WITH YOU, ROQUAT, IS YOU DON'T THINK CAREFULLY ENOUGH. *I DO!*
YOU'D MARCH THROUGH YOUR TUNNEL INTO OZ AND GET DEFEATED. *I WON'T!* I'LL HAVE A HOST OF ALLIES TO ASSIST MY NOMES.

THEY HAVEN'T MUCH OF AN ARMY IN OZ, BUT OZMA HAS A FAIRY WAND--DOROTHY HAS YOUR MAGIC BELT--AND THE SORCERESS GLINDA COMMANDS THE SPIRITS OF THE AIR.

AND I'VE HEARD THERE'S A WIZARD WHO'S SO SKILLFUL THAT PEOPLE USED TO PAY MONEY IN AMERICA TO SEE HIM PERFORM.

IT WILL BE NO EASY THING TO OVERCOME ALL THIS MAGIC.

WE HAVE FIFTY THOUSAND SOLDIERS!

NOMES ARE IMMORTAL, BUT NOT STRONG ON MAGIC. THE GREATER PART OF YOUR POWER WAS LOST WITH YOUR BELT.

BUT THERE ARE MANY EVIL CREATURES WITH MAGIC POWER SUFFICIENT TO DESTROY THE LAND OF OZ!

WE'LL GET THEM ON OUR SIDE AND TAKE OZ BY SURPRISE!

GUPH, YOU'RE THE GREATEST GENERAL I'VE EVER HAD! GO AT ONCE AND MAKE ARRANGEMENTS WITH THE EVIL POWERS TO ASSIST US--MEANTIME I'LL BEGIN TO DIG THE TUNNEL!

I'LL START THIS VERY AFTERNOON TO VISIT THE CHIEF OF THE WHIMSIES.

DOROTHY GALE LIVED ON A FARM IN KANSAS.

...OHHHH ...SNIFF--

AUNT EM! WHY ARE YOU CRYING?

...OHHH...

UNCLE HENRY, WHAT'S THE MATTER?

WE HAVEN'T TOLD YOU THE SAD NEWS, NOT WISHING TO MAKE YOU UNHAPPY--BUT WE MUST GIVE UP THE FARM, MY DEAR, AND GO AWAY SOMEWHERE TO EARN A LIVING.

WE'VE GROWN POORER EVERY YEAR, AND THE MORTGAGE COULDN'T BE PAID. NOW THE BANK SAYS I MUST PAY OR LEAVE THE FARM, BUT I CAN'T POSSIBLY GET THE MONEY.

WE DON'T MIND FOR OURSELVES, BUT WE'RE HEART-BROKEN TO THINK YOU MUST ENDURE POVERTY AND WORK FOR A LIVING BEFORE YOU'VE GROWN.

WHAT COULD I DO TO EARN MONEY?

YOU MIGHT DO HOUSEWORK-- OR BE A NURSE- MAID TO LITTLE CHILDREN--

WOULDN'T IT BE FUNNY FOR ME TO DO HOUSEWORK IN KANSAS, WHEN I'M A PRINCESS IN THE LAND OF OZ?

A PRINCESS!

YES, OZMA MADE ME A PRINCESS, AND SHE'S OFTEN BEGGED ME TO COME AND LIVE ALWAYS IN THE EMERALD CITY.

DO...DO YOU S'POSE...YOU COULD MANAGE TO RETURN TO YOUR FAIRYLAND, MY DEAR?

EASILY! OZMA SEES ME WHEREVER I AM EVERY FRIDAY AT FOUR O'CLOCK IN HER MAGIC PICTURE.

IF I MAKE A CERTAIN SIGN, SHE'LL SEND FOR ME BY MEANS OF THE MAGIC BELT. THEN, IN THE WINK OF AN EYE, I'LL BE WITH OZMA IN HER PALACE.

DOROTHY, YOU'D BETTER GO AND LIVE IN THE EMERALD CITY. IT'LL BREAK OUR HEARTS TO LOSE YOU, BUT YOU'LL BE MUCH BETTER OFF.

THESE THINGS SEEM REAL TO DOROTHY, I KNOW--

--BUT I'M AFRAID OUR LITTLE GIRL WON'T FIND HER FAIRYLAND JUST WHAT SHE'S DREAMED IT TO BE.

IT'S FRIDAY AND NEARLY FOUR O'CLOCK. PROMISE NOT TO WORRY, AND I'LL GO TO THE LAND OF OZ THIS AFTERNOON.

AND I PROMISE YOU'LL SEE ME AGAIN BEFORE YOU MUST LEAVE THIS FARM.

GO ON, TOTO--UPSTAIRS-- UP TO MY BEDROOM! COME ALONG, EUREKA.

*T*HEY WAITED.

DONG! DONG! DONG! DONG! DONG!

AND WAITED.

IT'S ALMOST FOUR-THIRTY.

I'M TOO IMPATIENT TO WAIT ANY LONGER.

DOROTHY? DOROTHY?

THE ROOM'S EMPTY.

OZMA'S ROYAL PALACE IN THE EMERALD CITY.

DOROTHY, MY DEAR!

OZMA! HOW GOOD TO SEE YOU!

WHAT'S THE MATTER? YOUR FACE WAS VERY SOBER WHEN I SAW IT IN MY MAGIC PICTURE.

UNCLE HENRY AND AUNT EM ARE IN A HEAP OF TROUBLE. THE BANK'S GOING TO TAKE THE FARM, AND THEY HAVE NO PLACE TO LIVE, UNLESS--

UNLESS WHAT, DEAR?

WELL, I'D LIKE TO LIVE HERE IN THE LAND OF OZ, WHERE YOU'VE OFTEN INVITED ME TO LIVE--BUT I CAN'T, UNLESS UNCLE HENRY AND AUNT EM COULD LIVE HERE, TOO.

SO, IN ORDER TO GET YOU, MY FRIEND, WE MUST INVITE YOUR UNCLE AND AUNT TO LIVE IN OZ, ALSO!

OH, WILL YOU BRING THEM HERE WITH THE MAGIC BELT, OZMA?

TO BE SURE. FOR *YOUR* FRIENDS, PRINCESS, THERE IS ALWAYS ROOM IN THE LAND OF OZ.

YOU MUSTN'T CALL ME "PRINCESS"--I'LL LIVE ON A NICE LITTLE FARM IN OZ--IN THE MUNCHKIN COUNTRY OR THE WINKIE COUNTRY--WITH UNCLE HENRY AND AUNT EM.

PRINCESS DOROTHY WILL NOT. YOU'RE GOING TO LIVE IN YOUR OWN ROOMS IN THIS PALACE AND BE MY COMPANION.

WE MUST FIND A PLACE FOR YOUR UNCLE AND AUNT WHERE THEY'LL BE COMFORTABLE AND NEEDN'T WORK.

I'M NOT SURE THEY BELIEVE IN THE LAND OF OZ, THOUGH I'VE TOLD THEM ABOUT IT LOTS OF TIMES.

THEY'LL BELIEVE IT WHEN THEY SEE IT. BUT IF THEY'RE TOLD THEY ARE TO MAKE A MAGICAL JOURNEY IT MAY MAKE THEM NERVOUS.

I THINK THE BEST WAY WILL BE TO USE THE MAGIC BELT TO BRING THEM HERE WITHOUT ANY WARNING--WHEN THEY'VE ARRIVED YOU CAN EXPLAIN WHATEVER THEY DON'T UNDERSTAND.

I'LL ORDER THE PALACE HOUSE-KEEPER TO HAVE ROOMS PREPARED. TOMORROW AFTER BREAKFAST WE'LL TRANSPORT YOUR AUNT AND UNCLE TO THE EMERALD CITY.

PERHAPS THAT'S BEST. THERE ISN'T MUCH USE IN THEIR STAYING AT THE FARM UNTIL THEY'RE PUT OUT--IT'S MUCH NICER HERE.

DOROTHY GALE, FROM THIS TIME FORTH YOU MUST ASSUME YOUR RIGHTFUL RANK AS A PRINCESS OF OZ.

AND BEING MY CHOSEN COMPANION--

--YOU MUST ACCEPT THIS CORONET AS BEFITTING THE DIGNITY OF YOUR POSITION.

THANK YOU, OZMA--ALTHOUGH I DON'T THINK THIS CAN MAKE ME ANYTHING ELSE THAN THE GIRL I'VE ALWAYS BEEN.

NOW, DEAR FRIEND, WE'LL TRANSPORT YOUR UNCLE AND AUNT FROM KANSAS.

P'RAPS WE'D BETTER GO INTO THE BACK YARD WHERE THE CABBAGES GROW--IT WOULD SEEM MORE NATURAL TO UNCLE HENRY AND AUNT EM.

NO, THEY SHALL FIRST SEE ME IN MY THRONE ROOM. ARE YOU READY, DOROTHY?

I AM-- BUT I DON'T KNOW WHETHER AUNT EM AND UNCLE HENRY ARE.

THE SOONER THEY BEGIN THEIR NEW LIFE HERE, THE HAPPIER THEY'LL BE. HERE THEY COME, MY DEAR!

WELL, I SWAN!

BY GUM!

D-D-D-DON'T THAT LOOK LIKE OUR LITTLE GIRL-- OUR DOROTHY, HENRY?

LOOK OUT, EM! TAKE CARE O' THE WILD BEASTS--OR YOU'RE A GONER!

DON'T BE AFRAID! YOU'RE IN THE LAND OF OZ, WHERE YOU'RE TO LIVE ALWAYS AND BE HAPPY! AND YOU OWE IT ALL TO THE KINDNESS OF MY FRIEND PRINCESS OZMA.

YOUR HIGHNESS, THIS IS UNCLE HENRY AND THIS IS AUNT EM.

YOU'RE VERY WELCOME HERE, WHERE I'VE BROUGHT YOU FOR PRINCESS DOROTHY'S SAKE.

I PRESENT TO MY PEOPLE OUR PRINCESS DOROTHY'S BELOVED UNCLE HENRY AND AUNT EM, HEREAFTER SUBJECTS OF OUR KINGDOM. SHOW THEM EVERY KINDNESS AND HONOR IN YOUR POWER.

I HOPE YOU'LL BE HAPPY IN YOUR NEW HOME.

IS IT ALL REAL? ARE WE TO STAY HERE?

DOROTHY WILL SHOW YOU TO THE ROOMS PREPARED FOR YOU. I HOPE YOU WILL LIKE THEM AND I'LL EXPECT YOU TO JOIN ME AT LUNCHEON.

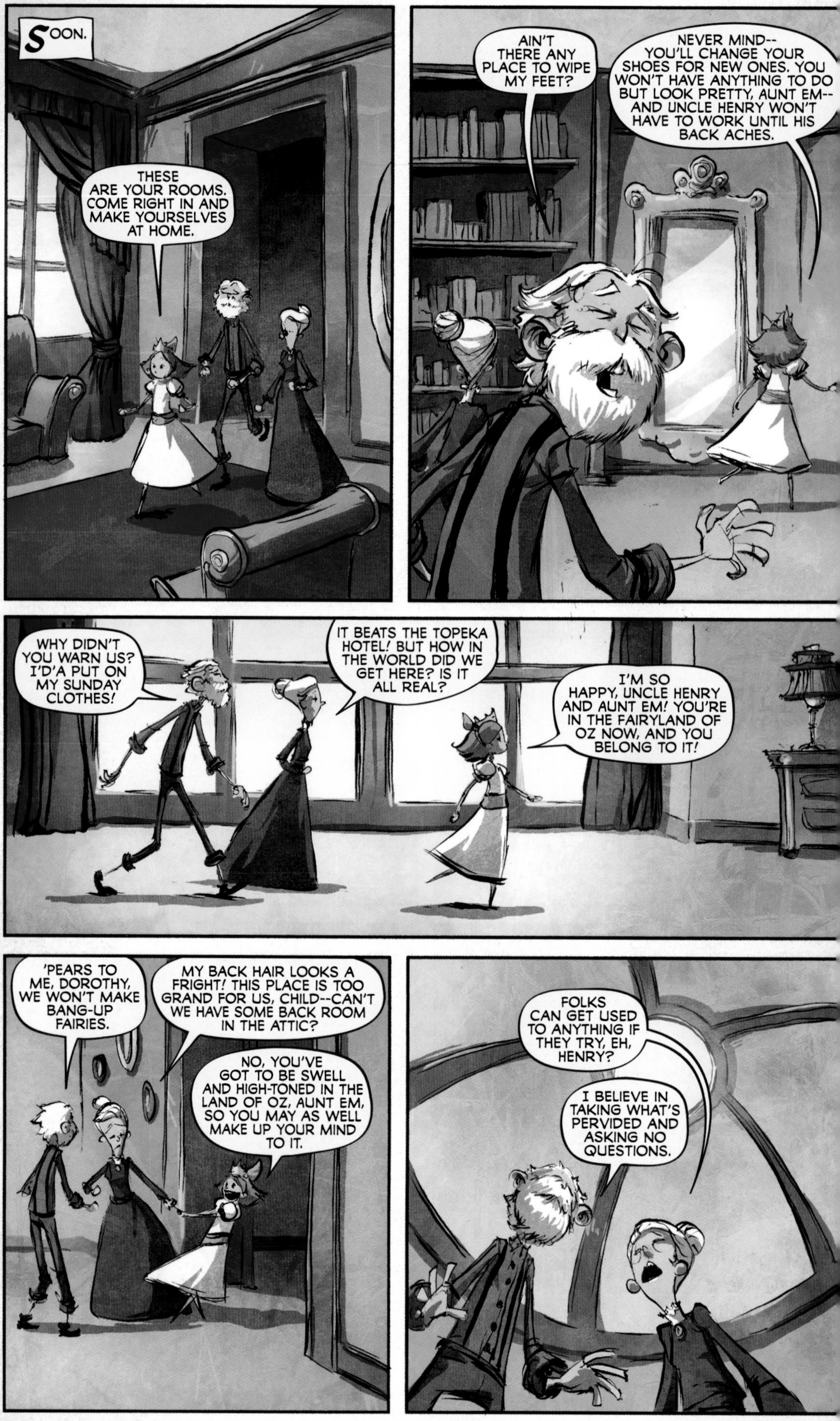
SOON.
THESE ARE YOUR ROOMS. COME RIGHT IN AND MAKE YOURSELVES AT HOME.
AIN'T THERE ANY PLACE TO WIPE MY FEET?
NEVER MIND-- YOU'LL CHANGE YOUR SHOES FOR NEW ONES. YOU WON'T HAVE ANYTHING TO DO BUT LOOK PRETTY, AUNT EM-- AND UNCLE HENRY WON'T HAVE TO WORK UNTIL HIS BACK ACHES.
WHY DIDN'T YOU WARN US? I'D'A PUT ON MY SUNDAY CLOTHES!
IT BEATS THE TOPEKA HOTEL! BUT HOW IN THE WORLD DID WE GET HERE? IS IT ALL REAL?
I'M SO HAPPY, UNCLE HENRY AND AUNT EM! YOU'RE IN THE FAIRYLAND OF OZ NOW, AND YOU BELONG TO IT!
'PEARS TO ME, DOROTHY, WE WON'T MAKE BANG-UP FAIRIES.
MY BACK HAIR LOOKS A FRIGHT! THIS PLACE IS TOO GRAND FOR US, CHILD--CAN'T WE HAVE SOME BACK ROOM IN THE ATTIC?
NO, YOU'VE GOT TO BE SWELL AND HIGH-TONED IN THE LAND OF OZ, AUNT EM, SO YOU MAY AS WELL MAKE UP YOUR MIND TO IT.
FOLKS CAN GET USED TO ANYTHING IF THEY TRY, EH, HENRY?
I BELIEVE IN TAKING WHAT'S PERVIDED AND ASKING NO QUESTIONS.

*R*OQUAT THE RED SET A THOUSAND NOME MINERS TO WORK.

RUN THE TUNNEL CLEAR THROUGH TO THE EMERALD CITY! IF MY ARMIES APPEAR ABOVE GROUND IN THE WINKIE COUNTY, OZMA WILL FORTIFY THE CITY AND ASSEMBLE AN ARMY!

GENERAL GUPH STARTED OUT TO VISIT THE WHIMSIES.

THESE WHIMSIES ARE FOOLISH ENOUGH TO IMAGINE THAT NO ONE SUSPECTS THEIR PASTE-BOARD IMITATION HEADS CONCEAL THEIR REAL HEADS WHICH ARE NO BIGGER THAN DOOR-KNOBS.

"OF COURSE, SUCH TINY HEADS CAN'T CONTAIN ANY GREAT AMOUNT OF BRAINS-- THEY DON'T KNOW IT'S FOLLY TO TRY TO APPEAR OTHERWISE THAN AS NATURE HAS MADE US."

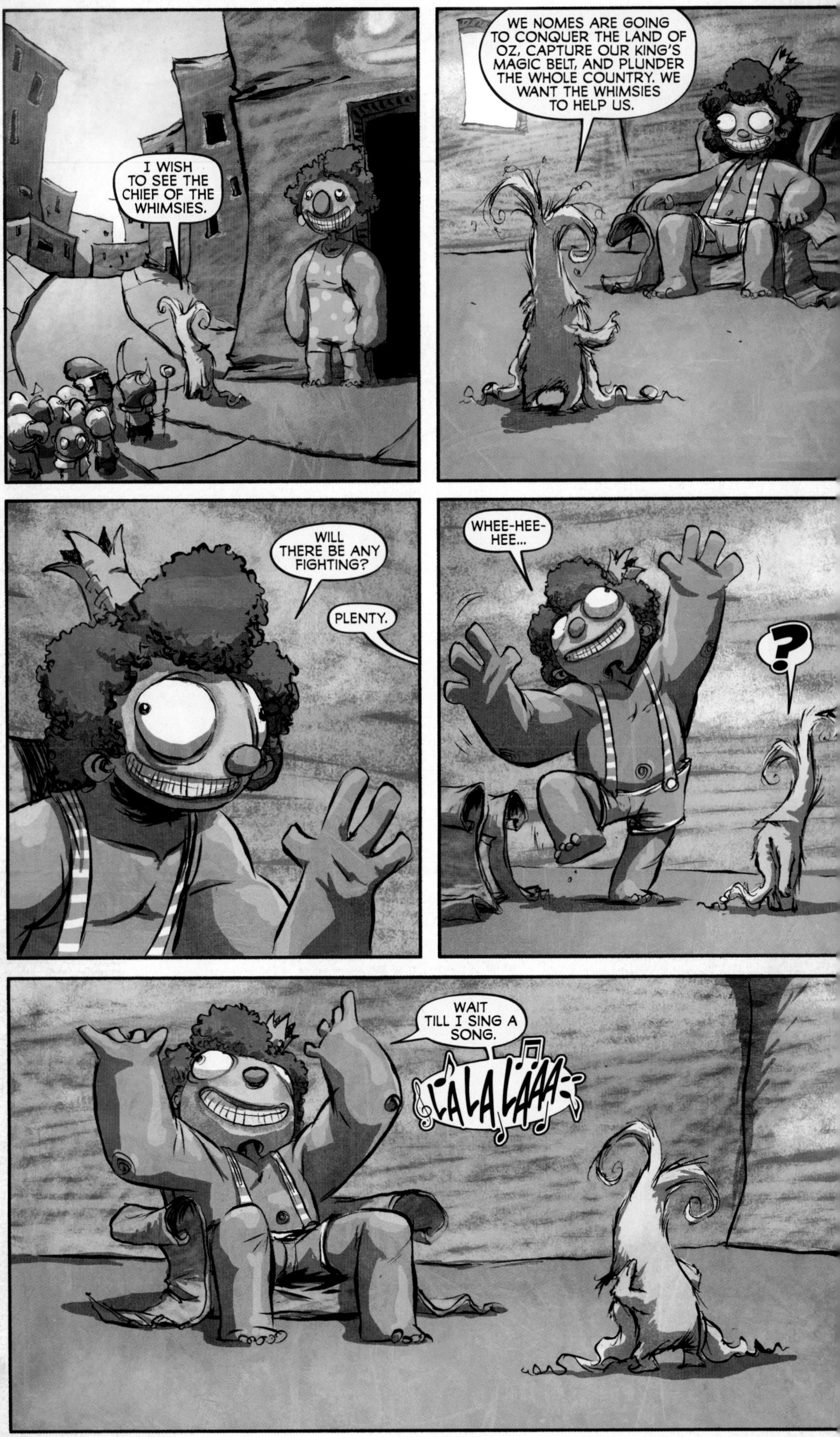
I WISH TO SEE THE CHIEF OF THE WHIMSIES.
WE NOMES ARE GOING TO CONQUER THE LAND OF OZ, CAPTURE OUR KING'S MAGIC BELT, AND PLUNDER THE WHOLE COUNTRY. WE WANT THE WHIMSIES TO HELP US.
WILL THERE BE ANY FIGHTING?
PLENTY.
WHEE-HEE-HEE...
?
WAIT TILL I SING A SONG.
LA LA LAAA

WHAT REWARD WILL YOU GIVE US IF WE HELP?

KING ROQUAT WILL USE HIS MAGIC BELT TO GIVE EVERY WHIMSIE A NATURAL HEAD AS BIG AND FINE AS THE FALSE HEAD HE NOW WEARS.

OH! WILL YOU DO THAT?

WE SURELY WILL.

THE CHIEF CALLED A MEETING OF ALL THE WHIMSIES.

--AND WE WILL NO LONGER BE ASHAMED THAT OUR BIG, STRONG BODIES HAVE SUCH TEENTY-WEENTY HEADS!

WE'LL FIGHT FOR THE NOMES!

WE'LL CONQUER OZ!

COLLECT THEM ALL!

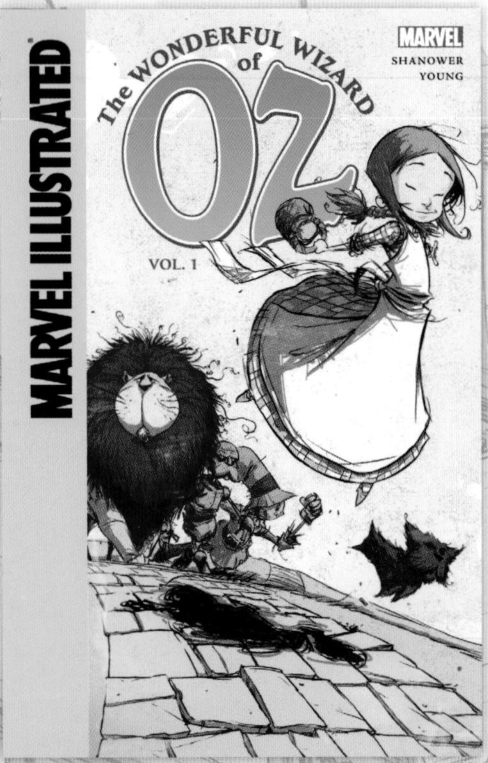
MARVEL ILLUSTRATED
MARVEL
SHANOWER
YOUNG
The WONDERFUL WIZARD of OZ
VOL. 1

The Wonderful Wizard of Oz
Set of 8 books: 978-1-61479-225-3

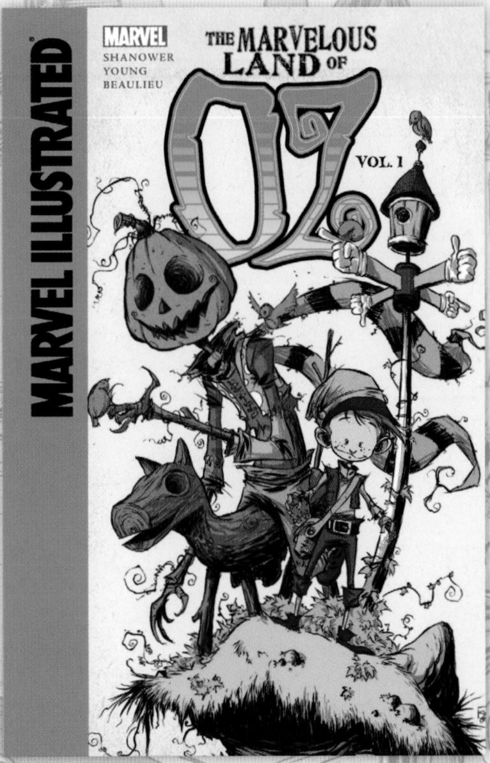
MARVEL ILLUSTRATED
MARVEL
SHANOWER
YOUNG
BEAULIEU
THE MARVELOUS LAND OF OZ
VOL. 1

The Marvelous Land of Oz
Set of 8 books: 978-1-61479-234-5

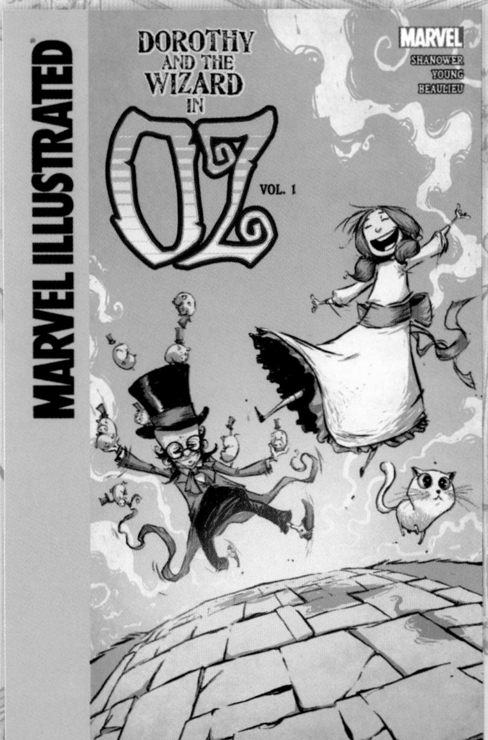
MARVEL ILLUSTRATED
MARVEL
SHANOWER
YOUNG
BEAULIEU
DOROTHY AND THE WIZARD IN OZ
VOL. 1

Dorothy and the Wizard in Oz
Set of 8 books: 978-1-61479-342-7

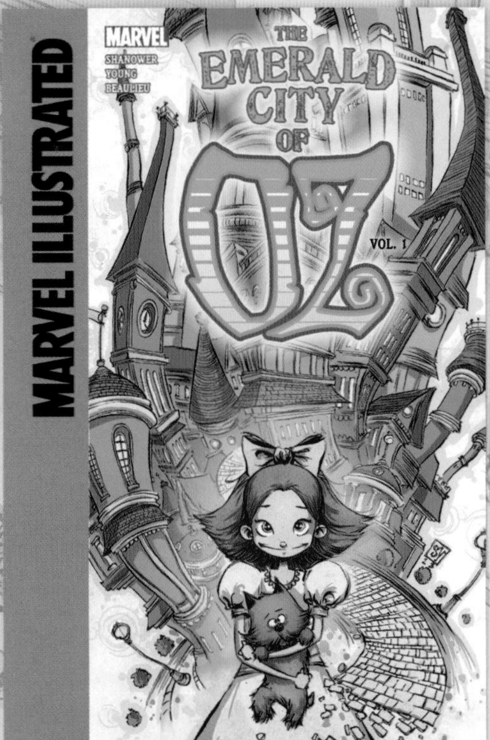
MARVEL ILLUSTRATED
MARVEL
SHANOWER
YOUNG
BEAULIEU
THE EMERALD CITY OF OZ
VOL. 1

The Emerald City of Oz
Set of 5 books: 978-1-61479-351-9